No Luck!

By
Josie Stewart
and Lynn Salem
Illustrations by Kristine Dillard

Dad and I were playing catch.
My frisbee got stuck in the tree.
Dad tried to get it down with a stick.
No luck!

Mom tried to get it down.
She threw a football. No luck!

3

My Grandpa tried to get it down.
He threw his golf club.

The pizza man tried to get it down.
No luck!

My brother tried to get it down
with his shoe.

Mr. Jones tried to get it down.
No luck!

Mr. Jones' dog tried to get it down.

He chased the cat up the tree.

The stick came down.
The football came down.
The golf club came down.

The shoe came down.
My frisbee came down at last.

But, the cat…no luck!